Walt Disney's

MICKEY MOUSE'S
PIC

STORY BY JANE WERNER
ILLUSTRATIONS BY THE WALT DISNEY STUDIO

GOLDEN PRESS • NEW YORK
Western Publishing Company, Inc.
Racine, Wisconsin

This Little Golden Book was produced under the supervision of

THE WALT DISNEY STUDIO

a b c d e f g h i j

Mickey Mouse sang.

"What a beautiful day for a picnic,
What a picnical day for a lark!
We will frolic all day
In the happiest way,
And we won't get back home until dark!"

Mickey was feeling very happy as he skipped up the walk to Minnie Mouse's house.

"Ready, Minnie?" he called.

Pluto and Goofy and Daisy Duck and Clarabelle Cow were waiting in Mickey's car.

"Ready!" smiled Minnie. Mickey peeked inside the lunch basket. Minnie had packed

peanut butter and jelly sandwiches and
cold meat sandwiches and
deviled eggs and potato salad,
radishes and onions and
pink lemonade and
a great big chocolate cake!

"Let's go!" said Mickey. And he picked up the basket and led Minnie out to the car.

"It seems strange to start off on a picnic without Donald Duck," said Mickey as they drove away.

"Yes, but there is always trouble when Donald is along," said the others.

None of them saw a figure watching from behind the bushes. And when they were far down the road, none of them saw that figure come out from hiding and jump up and down in rage!

"What a beautiful day for a picnic,
What a picnical day for a lark!"

everyone sang as Mickey Mouse drove merrily down the road to the picnic grounds.

And it did start out to be a perfect day. First they went for a walk along the river bank. They found a grassy spot beneath a tall shade tree. And they left Minnie's lunch basket there.

Then everyone went swimming in the old swimming hole. And how good that fresh, cool water felt! They swam and floated and played around, and had a wonderful time.

"I'm hungry enough to eat that whole basketful of lunch myself," Mickey Mouse said after a while.

"We'll see that you don't, Mickey Mouse!" Minnie laughed. "But it is time to eat, I guess."

So they all scrambled out of the water and hurried off to dress.

"Say!" Goofy cried. "Look at this, will you!"

Goofy was holding up his pants. The legs were all tied into knots. So were his shirt sleeves. And Mickey's were, too.

"Well, I never!" said Clarabelle Cow.

"Some mischief maker must be around," Mickey said, with a shake of his head.

But Minnie had a worse thought than that.

"The lunch!" she cried. And she ran up the bank to the shade of that big old tree.

The lunch basket was gone!

"Oh!" groaned everyone. "Not the lunch!"

"Hurry into your clothes, everybody!" Mickey cried. "We'll soon find out about this."

They struggled to undo the knots in their clothes. Then they dressed in a flash and were off on the hunt.

All through the woods they hunted, under every bush and trailing vine. But not a sign of that lunch basket did they see.

At last they came out on the road again, near where they had left Mickey's car. They were hot and tired and hungry and cross.

And it was then that they met Donald Duck, walking along the road all by himself. He had a fishing pole over one shoulder. And a bundle hung from the end of the fishing pole.

Donald was whistling as he walked along, and he looked very pleased with himself.

"Well, hello, hello, hello!" he cried. "Imagine meeting you folks out here. I just came for some fishing myself. Got tired of spending a lonely day at home."

"Oh—er—yes," said Mickey. He felt bad because they had left Donald behind.

"Where are you folks going?" Donald asked.

"We are hunting for our lunch," Mickey said.

"For lunch?" said Donald. "Why, I have enough for us all in my bundle here. I will be glad to share it with my friends."

Now everyone felt guilty. But they were hungry, so they said thank you, they would like to eat with Donald.

Under the same big shady tree Donald opened his bundle and spread out his lunch.

It was delicious. There were
peanut butter and jelly sandwiches and
cold meat sandwiches and
deviled eggs and potato salad,
radishes and onions and
pink lemonade and
a great big chocolate cake!

A strange look came into Mickey and Minnie Mouse's eyes as they saw that picnic lunch. But they did not say a word.

So they all sat down and ate and ate.

"This is delicious, Donald," said Clarabelle Cow.

"And it is nice of you, too, Donald," Daisy Duck added, "to share it with us."

"Sure is," said Goofy, reaching for another sandwich.

"Yes," Mickey admitted. "I guess we misjudged you, Donald, old boy."

"Humph!" said Minnie Mouse. Then she turned to Donald with her sweetest smile.

"Did you bring a knife for cutting the chocolate cake, Donald?" she asked.

"Er—ah, I had one somewhere," Donald said. He looked all around. But he could not find it.

"I fastened a knife to the bottom of my cake pan with paper tape," Minnie said.

Mickey leaned over and looked at the bottom of the cake pan. And there, sure enough, was a knife, fastened to the bottom of the pan with paper tape. On the knife handle were the letters M. M.

"Well!" said Minnie.

"Why, Donald!" cried Daisy Duck.

"So that's where our lunch disappeared to," cried Mickey.

Donald dropped his eyes. "I'm sorry, honest I am," he said. "I won't ever do it again."

"And where is my lunch basket?" Minnie asked.

"In the back of Mickey's car," Donald admitted.

Mickey had to laugh. "Well," he said, as he cut the cake, "we've all learned a lesson, I think. Donald won't snatch any lunch baskets soon. And we know it's better to bring Donald on a picnic."

Everyone had to laugh then. And they all piled back into Mickey's car. They made room for Donald to sit in the empty lunch basket.

Then away they went toward town, singing merrily:

"We will frolic all day
In the happiest way,
And we won't get back home until dark!"